THE MYSTERIOUS
VALENTINE

• *Louanne Pig in* •

THE MYSTERIOUS
VALENTINE

Nancy Carlson

Carolrhoda Books, Inc. ♦ Minneapolis

This book is available in two editions:
Library binding by Carolrhoda Books, Inc.
Soft cover by First Avenue Editions
c/o The Lerner Group
241 First Avenue North
Minneapolis, Minnesota 55401

LIBRARY OF CONGRESS CATALOGING IN PUBLICATION DATA

Carlson, Nancy L.
    Louanne Pig in the mysterious valentine.

    Title on added t.p.: The mysterious valentine.
    Summary: When she receives a valentine from a
secret admirer, Louanne Pig tries to find out who
sent it.
    1. Children's stories, American. [1. Pigs—
Fiction. 2. Valentines—Fiction.] I. Title. II. Title:
Mysterious valentine.
PZ7.C21665Lk 1985   [E]   85-3757
    ISBN 0-87614-282-X (lib. bdg.)
    ISBN 1-57505-032-3 (pbk.)

Manufactured in the United States of America
    6 7 8 9 10 – P/JP – 02 01 00 99 98 97

On February 14, Louanne looked in the mailbox and found the most beautiful valentine she'd ever seen. It was addressed to her!

Louanne raced inside.

"Look what I got!" she screamed. "A valentine from a secret admirer...

I wonder who it's from."
"Eat your pancakes," said Dad.

On the way to school, Louanne showed her valentine to Harriet.

"Wow!" said Harriet. "That's the biggest valentine I've ever seen! Do you know who sent it?"

"Well, I know one thing about him," said
Louanne. "He has a green pen. Look at the
signature."

All through her math lesson, Louanne thought about her valentine.

All through her geography lesson, she
thought about the green pen. By the time her
art lesson began, Louanne was determined to
track down her secret admirer.

Maybe it's George, she thought. She peered over his shoulder. There was a blue pen on his desk, and a red pen too, and three chewed-up pencils. But there was no green pen.

"Hey, potato breath," said George, "quit breathing on me."

"Sorry," Louanne mumbled. She was glad it wasn't George.

Right before recess, Louanne got another
idea. It must be Arnie, she thought.

She waited until everyone else had left the room. Then she crept over to Arnie's desk and peeked inside. There were three crayons, two paintbrushes, and five pencils sharpened to perfect points—but no green pen.

"What do you think you're doing!" yelled
Arnie from the doorway.

"Er...I needed a green pen," said Louanne.

"A likely story!" said Arnie. "You were probably after my candy bar." He grabbed the candy bar and marched out.

"I'm glad *you're* not my secret admirer," Louanne mumbled after him.

At lunch, Louanne checked Doug's pocket.
No green pen there.

That was just as well, she thought.

She checked Harold's book bag.

There was no green pen there either. That
was a relief.

After school, she even asked Big Mike if
he had a green pen.

"No way, pig!" he shouted at her. "What's
it to you, anyway."

"Whew!" Louanne sighed as she made her
escape. "I sure am glad it's not Big Mike!"

On her way home, Louanne stopped in at the card shop.

"Excuse me, sir," she said to the clerk. "You don't happen to remember who bought this valentine, do you?"

"I sure do," said the clerk. "He was a big
fellow with a curly tail."

"Do you remember his name?" Louanne asked excitedly.

"Sorry," said the clerk. "He never mentioned his name."

Louanne thought about the clerk's description all the way home. The trouble was, she didn't *know* any big fellows with curly tails.

"I give up," she told her dad. "I can't figure out *who* sent me this valentine. All I can figure out is who I'm glad *didn't* send it."

"I guess it's just meant to be a mystery,"
said her dad.

"I guess so," said Louanne. "I wonder if
I'll get one next year."